Whose Hat?

by Margaret Miller

Greenwillow Books, New York

The photographs were reproduced in full color
from 35 mm Kodachrome slides.
The typeface is Avant Garde Gothic.

Printed in Singapore by Tien Wah Press
First Edition   10 9 8 7 6 5

Library of Congress Cataloging-in-Publication Data
Miller, Margaret (date)   Whose hat?
Summary: Presents color photographs of hats that represent
various occupations including a chef's cap, construction
worker's helmet, magician's hat, and a fire fighter's hat.
1. Hats—Juvenile literature.   [1. Hats]   I. Title.
GT2110.M55   1988   391.43   86-18324
ISBN 0-688-06906-1
ISBN 0-688-06907-X (lib. bdg.)

For Jacob,
my favorite hat collector

Whose hat?

Chef

Whose hat?

Fire fighter

Whose hat?

Pirate

Whose hat?

Construction worker

Whose hat?

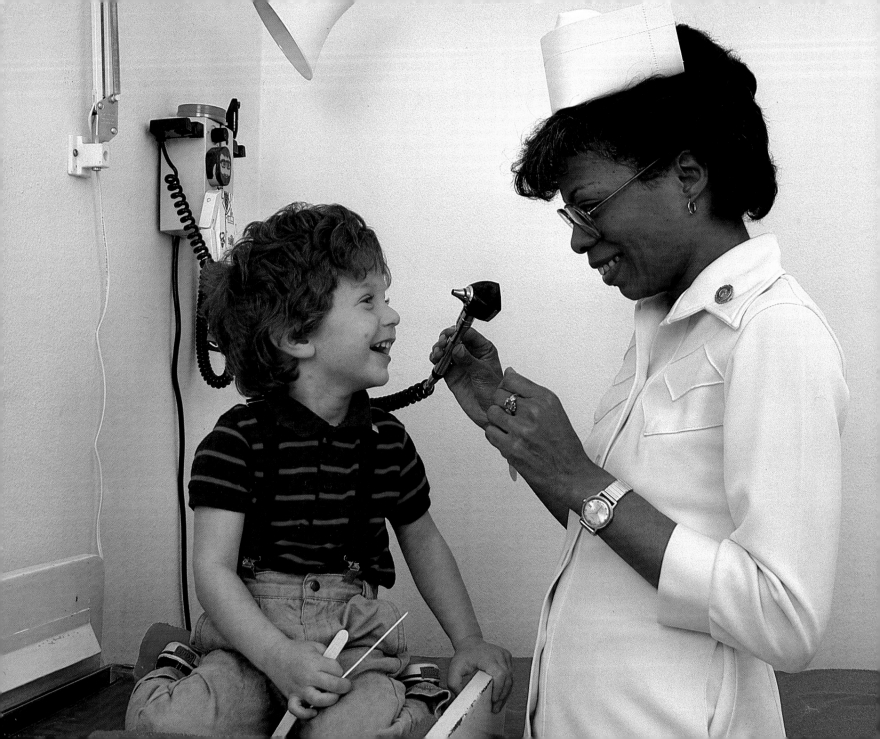

Nurse

Whose hat ?

Police officer

Whose hat ?

Cow hand

Whose hat ?

Magician

Whose hat?

Witch

MARGARET MILLER is a freelance photographer who lives in New York City with her husband, two children, two dogs, and many hats. She traces her love of photography to her childhood. "My mother is a wonderful photographer, and as a child I loved being with her in the mysterious darkroom. I also spent many hours looking through two very powerful books, The Family of Man edited by Edward Steichen, and You Have Seen Their Faces by Erskine Caldwell and Margaret Bourke-White. After college I worked in children's book publishing for a number of years, but then took time off to have our two children. As the children grew older and I had more free time, I returned to photography."

Margaret Miller's previous books include Hot Off the Press!, A Day at the Daily News, and Rat-a-Tat Pitterpat.